Hello Parents

Hooray! Your child is starting to read.
A whole new world is opening up,
word by word and page by page.

Hello Kitty is the perfect companion for
beginner readers. In these seven simple
stories, she takes your child along on her
adventure—playing baseball, baking cookies,
even traveling across the USA!

The first three stories in this volume are
Level 1, just right for children who know
the alphabet and want to start reading.

The last four stories are Level 2, perfect for
new readers who are familiar with basic words
and can sound out new words with help.

Hello Kitty®

Stories of Fun and Friends

Level 1 and Level 2 Books
A Collection of Seven Early Readers

Abrams Books for Young Readers, New York

CONTENTS

Hello Kitty®
Visits Grandma!

Level 1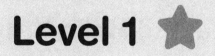

Grandma and Hello Kitty.

Big hugs.

Time to paint.

Flowers!

Time for lunch!

Look at the clouds!

Grandma and Hello Kitty stitch.

Time to cook.

Yum, yum.

Cake!

Dress up!
Pretty Hello Kitty!

Look at Grandma in a balloon.
Look at Grandma in a plane.

The cake is done.

Time to eat.

Yum, yum.

Tea party.

Teddy joins the fun.

Hello Kitty eats popcorn.

Time to go home.

Good-bye Grandma!

Good-bye Grandpa!

Hello Kitty®
Hello Love!

Level 1 ⭐

Hello Kitty and Daniel.

Special friends!

It is Daniel's birthday.

What will Hello Kitty give Daniel?

Flowers?

A bee?

A rainbow?

Fifi and Hello Kitty love butterflies.

But they are hard to wrap!

A sailboat for Daniel?

Five fishes? Too wet!

Timmy and Tammy say
to give Daniel birds.
But birds fly away!

Hello Kitty asks Moley.

An umbrella for Daniel?

No, he has an umbrella.

Hello Kitty sits on pillows.

She thinks and thinks.

Hello Kitty has a good idea!

She works with Kathy, Joey,
Moley, and Timmy and
Tammy.

Daniel's present is a garden.

He loves it!

Hello Kitty®
A Day with Papa

Level 1

Hello Kitty and Papa spend the day together.

"What shall we do?" Papa asks.

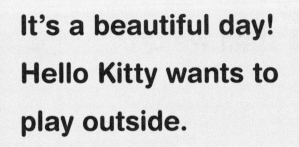

It's a beautiful day!
Hello Kitty wants to
play outside.

"We can play baseball," says Papa.

Hello Kitty writes a note for Mama and Mimmy.

Hello Kitty and Papa

walk to the store.

They pick baseball
gloves and balls.

They buy a baseball shirt
and a baseball bat.

Hello Kitty loves to shop!

Papa says it is important to wear a helmet.

Hello Kitty chooses a
pink helmet.

Papa shows Hello Kitty how
to swing the bat.
Hello Kitty hits the ball.

Then Hello Kitty catches the ball.

Hello Kitty and Papa play catch
until they are hungry.

Hot dogs for lunch! Yum!

Hello Kitty sees Joey, Fifi, Jody, and Kathy in the park.

"Let's play a game of baseball!"

Joey pitches to Hello Kitty.

She hits a home run.

"Hooray!"

Hello Kitty and Papa walk home.

"I love baseball!" says Hello Kitty.

Hello Kitty®
A Surprise for Mama

Level 2 ⭐ ⭐

Hello Kitty and Mimmy are excited.

They have a surprise for Mama.

"Let's bake cookies," says Hello Kitty

"Mama loves sugar cookies."

"We need flour and sugar,"
says Mimmy.

"We need eggs and
butter," says Hello Kitty.
"We do not need fish!" says Mimmy.

Hello Kitty mixes the sugar and flour.

Baking is fun!

"I will crack the eggs,"
says Hello Kitty.

"Eggs are messy."

Mama helps Hello Kitty and Mimmy.

It's fun to bake with Mama.

Mimmy rolls the cookies.

Hello Kitty cuts star shapes.

Mama puts the cookies in the oven.

Time to clean
the kitchen.
Everybody helps.

"The cookies smell good."

Hello Kitty and Mimmy decorate
with icing and sprinkles.

"We had fun!"

Mama hugs Hello Kitty and Mimmy.

Hello Kitty, Mimmy, and
Mama sit in the garden.

They eat cookies and drink milk.
Yum, yum.

Hello Kitty®
Loves School!

Level 2 ⭐ ⭐

Hello Kitty loves school.
There are so many things
to learn!

Fifi thinks science class is fun.

Hello Kitty's favorite class is English.

Hello Kitty and her friends take drama class.

They write and act in plays.

Everyone chooses an instrument
in music class.

Hello Kitty plays a song on the piano.

In gym class everyone
takes turns tumbling.

Let's Play Soccer

They run fast and jump high.
Joey does a cartwheel.

The talent show is always a success!

The friends get ready for the show.

Thomas and Mimmy perform a play.

Mimmy is a princess.

Joey helps.

Act 1

The crowd cheers!

Fifi mixes a potion and makes bubbles.

Act 2

Cathy reads her poem:

Flowers open in the sun

Petals close when day is done.

Act 3

Joey jumps through a hoop.

He scores a perfect 10.

For the end of the show
Hello Kitty plays the piano.

Her friends dance.

Finale

Everyone agrees this is
the best talent show ever.

Hooray!

Hello Kitty®
Graduation Day

Level 2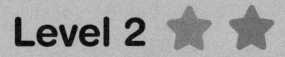

Hello Kitty is excited to graduate.

She writes a speech for
graduation day.

Then a strong wind scatters
her notes.
Thomas can't save the papers.

They blow everywhere!
Oh, no!

Hello Kitty has an idea
for a new speech.

She asks her friends and family
what she should say.

Grandpa White tells Hello Kitty to talk about what she has learned. He says, "You can play the piano!

You can read many books!"
"Be proud of yourself,"
says Grandma White.

"Remember to say that you are
strong and brave," says Mama.

Then Mama gives Hello Kitty a cookie.

Papa says, "You and your friends
have so many talents.

Talk about those in your speech."

"Thank your friends and teachers,"
says Mimmy.

"They help you work and play."

Hello Kitty talks to Thomas.

"Graduation day is a great reason
to have a party!" says Thomas.

Hello Kitty makes her graduation speech.

Everyone smiles and cheers.
Then they throw their caps
into the air.

The day ends with a party.

Everyone eats cookies and

drinks juice.

**Hello Kitty gives hugs
to all her friends.**

Hello Kitty®
Takes a Trip

Level 2 ⭐⭐

Hello Kitty is going on a trip.

She will drive across the country!

The first stop is New England.
This is where the pilgrims
first landed.

"Let's eat turkey and pie just like the pilgrims did!" says Hello Kitty.

Hello Kitty and Fifi get on a boat and sail in the Atlantic Ocean. The boat goes fast and the wind is strong!

Hello Newport

TIMES SQUARE

Hello Kitty visits New York City.

FASHION AVENUE

She sees the Empire State Building and the Statue of Liberty.

STOP

Hello Kitty and Fifi hike in the mountains.

"My backpack is heavy!"
says Hello Kitty.

157

Philadelphia is known as the birthplace of the nation.

Hello Kitty and her friends visit Independence Hall and eat cheesesteak sandwiches.

Washington, DC, is the capital of the U.S.A. "Let's visit the president!" says Hello Kitty.

161

Graceland, in Memphis, Tennessee, is the home of Elvis.

Hello Kitty loves to sing and dance to the music.

A trip to the spa means
it's time to rest.

Hello Kitty and Fifi take a dip in the hot springs to relax.

"Let's go the beach!"
says Hello Kitty.

"Bring your water pail and your sunscreen!" Hello Kitty rests under the palm trees.

A stop at the amusement park means spins, bumps, and loops!

Hello Kitty and her friends
ride the rollercoaster.

Mardi Gras is a big party held each year in New Orleans.

Hello Kitty is the queen of the parade and wears a pretty dress.

172

Hello Kitty learns cowboy stories in Texas.

"I love chili," says Hello Kitty. "It's yummy when it's cooked over a campfire!"

Visiting a farm is a chance to pick vegetables and meet farm animals.

Hello Kitty makes friends with the pigs and the cows.

The next stop is Chicago.
Hello Kitty visits the
Willis Tower, the tallest
building in the U.S.A.

Hello Kitty takes pictures of the city.

MALL OF AMERICA

Shopping is Hello Kitty's favorite hobby.

She buys gifts for Mama, Papa, and Mimmy.

When they leave the big city, Hello Kitty and her friends take a rafting trip down the river.

It's a wet and wild ride!

The deserts of the Southwest
are filled with pretty colors.

Hello Kitty rides a donkey through the Grand Canyon.

A hot-air balloon ride takes Hello
Kitty and Fifi high above the desert.

"This is the biggest
balloon I've ever seen,"
says Hello Kitty.

Hello Kitty learns to ski in the Rocky Mountains of Colorado.

She flips and leaps high in the air!

The Pacific Northwest
has huge green forests.

"This is where we get our apples, pears, and Christmas trees!" says Hello Kitty.

California is Hello Kitty's final stop.

In Hollywood Hello Kitty
pretends she's a famous
movie star. "Traveling is
fun!" says Hello Kitty.

ABRAMS
THE ART OF BOOKS SINCE 1949

115 West 18th Street
New York, NY 10011
www.abramsbooks.com